To Adrien and Massimo,
the bestest of friends
—LP

For Ivy, my universe
—SW

Text copyright © 2018 by Stephanie Watson
Illustrations copyright © 2018 by LeUyen Pham

All rights reserved. Published by Scholastic Press, an imprint of Scholastic Inc.. Publishers since 1920. SCHOLASTIC PRESS. SCHOLASTIC, and associated logos are trademarks and/or registered trademarks of Scholastic Inc.

Library of Congress Cataloging-in-Publication Data
Names: Watson. Stephanie. 1979- author. | Pham. LeUyen, illustrator.
Title: Best friends in the universe / [text by Stephanie Watson : Illustrations by LeUyen Pham].
Description: First edition. | New York. NY : Scholastic Press, 2018. | Summary: Hector and Louie are writing a book to explain the many reasons that they are the best friends in the universe—but will their friendship, and their book, survive when they start to reveal each other's secrets?
Identifiers: LCCN 2017049312 | ISBN 9780545659888 (hardcover)
Subjects: LCSH: Best friends—Juvenile fiction. | Books—Juvenile fiction. | Friendship—Fiction. | Books—Fiction. | Quarreling—Juvenile fiction. | CYAC: Best Friends—Fiction. | Friendship—Fiction. | Books—Fiction. | Quarreling—Fiction. | Secrets—Fiction.
Classification: LCC PZ7.W32949 Be 2018 | DDC [E]—dc23 LC record available at https://lccn.loc.gov/2017049312

10 9 8 7 6 5 4 3 2 1   18 19 20 21 22
First edition, October 2018

Printed in China 62
Book design by LeUyen Pham

The art for this book was rendered in pencil and crayon, and enhanced digitally in Photoshop.

70 ◎

70 ◎

2

⊕

⚒

100 ◎⊕

70

INTRODUCING . . .

BEST FRIENDS IN THE UNIVERSE

BY HECTOR and LOUIE

Scholastic Press • New York

TOP SECRET
Here's another reason why we're best friends:
We keep each other's secrets.
Like how one time, Louie wet his pants after too much peanut butter toast milkshake.

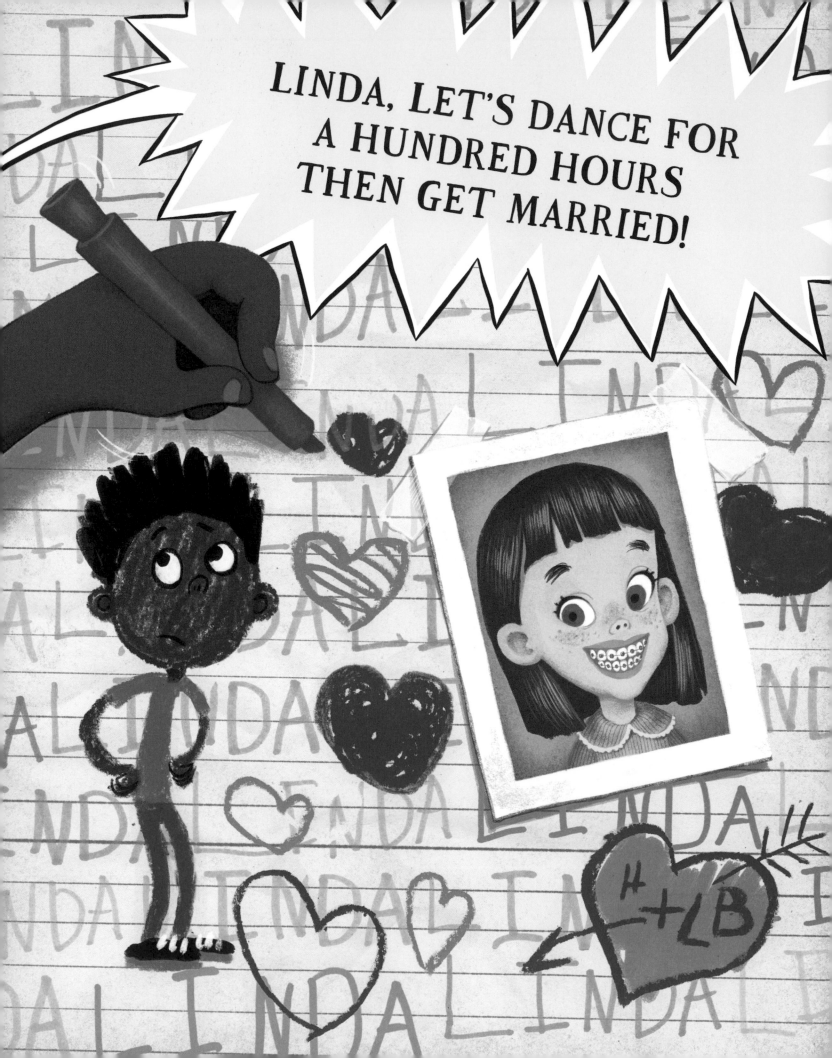

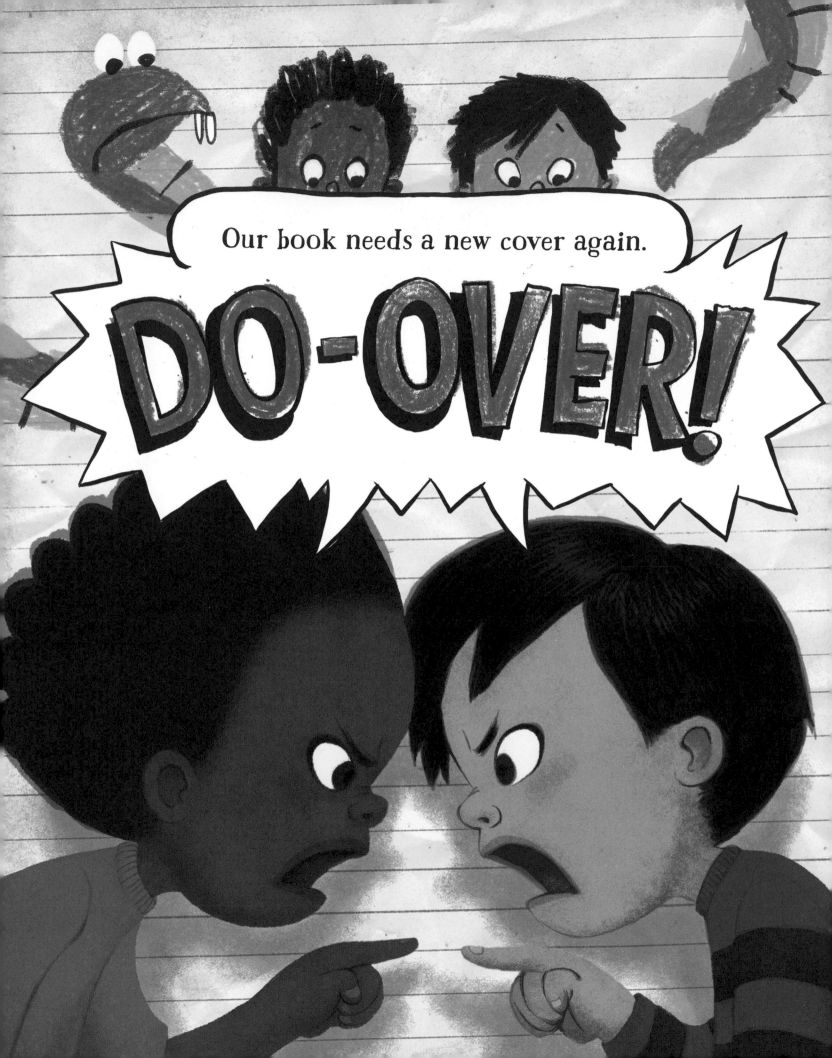

I'm going to make up an ugly dance move called The Horrible Hector.
I'm going to invent a disgusting, rotten drink called The Icky Louie.

My new best friend is Python. He knows how to keep secrets!
I'm gonna make my OWN book!

MY new best friend is Python. He could win the secret-keeping Olympics!
I'm gonna make my own book, TOO!
???